WAY OF THE ODYSSEY SHORT STORY COLLECTION VOLUME 1

CONNOR WHITELEY

No part of this book may be reproduced in any form or by any electronic or mechanical means. Including information storage, and retrieval systems, without written permission from the author except for the use of brief quotations in a book review.

This book is NOT legal, professional, medical, financial or any type of official advice.

Any questions about the book, rights licensing, or to contact the author, please email connorwhiteley@connorwhiteley.net

Copyright © 2024 CONNOR WHITELEY

All rights reserved.

DEDICATION
Thank you to all my readers without you I couldn't do what I love.

TREATY OF DEFEAT

Lawyer Elaine Cars's life would be changed forever today.

Elaine sat inside her little sterile white plastic cubicle on the very top floor of her major law firm on Earth. She loved how the cubicle was always so bright, wonderful and clean unlike so many other places on Earth.

A large black holographic computer and grey hovering desk was in front of her, and Elaine really liked how the black office chair she was sitting at supported her so much better than her old one on the lower levels. She had only gotten the job promotion yesterday so this was her first full day and she seriously loved the new job so far.

It was just brilliant.

She was surprised how her new office chair seemed to cradle her body like the amazing hugs her mother used to give her before the foul cancer took her away.

And the chair supported her back, arms and neck perfectly so that Elaine was really hoping to get rid of the constant aching of her muscles from the poorly designed chairs of the awful lower levels.

Elaine was a little unsure about the sterile whiteness of the cubicle because it was a little unnerving. There was no art, paintings or pictures at all on the walls and her new boss had said that she should only be focusing on her legal work and not silly artwork.

But Elaine had always loved art ever since she was a little kid. To her, art was a way of preserving the human culture, learning about others and seeing the world in a new light.

Elaine shook away the thought and simply focused on her black holographic computer that she was seriously impressed by.

Her old one on the lower levels was so old, full and glitchy that her boss had threatened to sack her three times in the past week because apparently her productivity wasn't high enough. It was only not high enough because of the damn glitchy computer.

Thankfully that shouldn't be a problem up here on this floor, and Elaine loved how as her fingers gently touched the black holographic keyboard, the holograms no longer zapped her like her old ones did.

Every single damn night Elaine used to have to put her fingertips in a tub of ice to stop the pain, the zapping was that painful, but hopefully that wouldn't be a problem now.

Elaine clicked on her computer and was surprised that her caseload was so small today.

When she was working on the lower floors, she used to work forty cases a day and mostly she failed a ton of clients like every single other lawyer on Earth but she liked to believe she tried her hardest on all her cases. It was only yesterday she had helped keep a family together so they weren't ripped apart, she had also helped a family get their innocent daughter off a murder charge and she had convicted a kidnapper.

She helped so many amazing people and that was why she loved her job so much but she wanted to help even more people.

"Welcome Elaine to the Top Criminal Division of Baring & Law," her computer said.

Elaine felt so excited to finally be able to access the top-secret and highly sensitive and dangerous cases that these legendary lawyers dealt with.

But when she went to click on her inbox she watched all her other cases disappear and she was only left with a single case.

She clicked on it.

It was really odd that it took a while for the case file to open and Elaine detected a subtle change in the air. The environmental systems on Earth were meant to be the best in the Imperium but now all she could smell was sugar, caramel and candyfloss. It was a wonderful smell if not a little strange, yet she did love the taste of salted caramel that formed on her tongue.

"Access granted," the computer said.

Elaine had no idea why she needed access to look at her own workload but she didn't care and she simply looked at the file.

She instantly frowned as she read the file. She was going to have to deal with a female Keres, a foul alien abomination that had committed an awful crime against humanity and the Imperium.

Elaine hated the Keres with a passion, they were always so rude, foul and just beasts when compared to humanity. And they were just freaks as well with their magic and Elaine shivered in fear.

It was a very well-known rule in the Imperium that humans should never ever mix with such awful creatures that were sadly allowed to roam around in the Imperium because of the Treaty of Defeat.

The only piece of comfort that Elaine and all of humanity got from the Treaty was that the Keres were certainly second-class citizens and they were to be discriminated against at every single chance that presented itself.

Elaine actually wasn't so sure that was fair or just or right but she was a lawyer now and it was her task to make sure this Keres scum plead guilty to charges of theft.

It was so damn annoying that this scum felt like she had the right to steal from superior humans. That was disgraceful and Elaine was so looking forward to punishing this alien beast.

But she couldn't help but feel like there was more

to this story and as much as she wanted to believe everything the Imperium said about the Keres.

She had actually never met one before and she couldn't help but believe there was a tiny chance they weren't everything the posters said they were.

But right now all Elaine was interested in was protecting humanity from the aliens.

***

Because the Keres were such foul, dangerous and awful creatures, Elaine was really glad they were kept in high-security areas of the law firm so she had to go through more security checkpoints than she cared to think about.

Elaine went down a very long black metal corridor with prison bars lining the corridor and the disgusting Keres prisoners were standing there looking so scared at her, with bright blue prison collars around their awful necks.

Elaine absolutely hated the Keres' appearance. They were humanoid in shape but their chests and waists were a lot thinner and their facial features were more angled and she might have even classed the very fit men handsome if they weren't alien scum.

All the Keres wore black prisoner uniforms that fit their very slim and spinney bodies very well.

Just like everyone else in the Imperium Elaine had lived through the War between humans and Keres, and just like the news reports said Elaine had to agree that the Keres were monsters.

The aliens burnt entire planets in the name of their Empire, they murdered every human they came over and they used their magic for such dark purposes that Elaine often turned off the news at night. All whilst humanity was being angelic, calm and wonderful.

They never killed a Keres that didn't deserve it.

Elaine kept walking down the long corridor until she reached the end of it where a steel door was that opened for her only. She went inside.

The interrogation room was perfect for the female Keres scum that sat on a cold metal chair and rested on her long thin arms on the metal table. Thankfully she was chained and Elaine was not going to order the guards to release her.

The Keres were way too dangerous for that. And Elaine just had to focus on how badly she wanted to protect her friends, family and species from these foul aliens.

As Elaine sat down on the icy cold chair and tucked it in, she had to admit she was surprised that the Keres female looked so scared, human and innocent.

Yet that was something else that the glorious Rex pointed out about the awful Keres, they were masters of fear and manipulation. Elaine couldn't dare allow herself to be manipulated by the alien.

She had to remain strong to protect her species. And all she needed to do was get a confession and then go.

"You are accused of theft," Elaine said.

The Keres looked at her. "Please. I didn't steal anything. The human gave it to me,"

Elaine laughed. "That's what they all say and we all know you Keres are thieves,"

The female Keres shook her head as Elaine got out her holo-slate and looked at the case notes she had made in the lift.

"You were found with two hundred Guards worth of technological gadgets that you stole from a merchant," Elaine said.

"No," the Keres said. "I bought that equipment fair and square. I showed the Justice the receipt and he logged it into evidence,"

Elaine nodded because she wasn't lying and there was a receipt.

"I know but the Treaty of Defeat made it clear. The law states that if a Keres buys something then it doesn't belong to Keres. And if the human wants it back then the Keres must give it back without refund,"

The Keres's foul lips thinned. "I know that but…"

Elaine just couldn't understand how this alien could understand the law and so willingly break it. That was why no one liked the Keres.

It wasn't exactly a confession and Elaine sadly knew it wouldn't make her bosses happy with her.

"It just isn't fair," she said.

Elaine stopped for a moment. She had been given this case to get a guilty verdict and she needed this piece of scum to confess, but she highly doubted she would get it if she didn't fake trust and liking this piece of criminal trash.

Elaine forced herself to smile and looked at the alien. All she needed to do was get the alien to trust her and confess to her crime completely.

"Why did you buy it then?" Elaine asked, trying to sound how she did with humans.

The Keres looked at her like Elaine was a good friend. Elaine really couldn't believe how this species had gotten so powerful if they broke laws and trusted so easily.

"It's my husband's birthday today so I was going to get him a special treat. He fought for the humans in the War and he had always loved those old holo-movies so I was hoping to record one for myself and show him. I have a degree in Keres Film Studies,"

Elaine forced herself not to shiver. The Glorious Rex had shown the Imperium what the Keres called "movies" and it was horrific. There was so much blood, murder and other things that she didn't even want to think about.

And apparently what humans called horror films were comedies to the Keres. That was how messed up the aliens were.

Elaine forced herself to nod and smile. "That's really nice of you. I wished my husband did that for me,"

She didn't have a husband but she had learnt over the years if you wanted to make someone trust you, tell them you were in a relationship. It worked every time.

"Thank you. So I saved for months and months and I travelled here on a cargo shuttle to get the equipment,"

Elaine frowned. "You came on a method of transport that wasn't a dedicated Keres flight?"

The female Keres frowned slightly. "Um, it wasn't that serious. I only wanted to cross into Imperial Space for a day and the Keres flights are two hundred times the price of a cargo shuttle,"

Elaine shook her head. "I'm sorry but the Treaty is clear. Keres can only come into Imperial Space if they board a dedicated Keres flight. It is illegal for you to come on any other transport method,"

The Keres frowned. "And yet you humans can use any method to come into our Empire. You can teleport, use cargo shuttles, tourist shuttles and military transports. How is that fair?"

Elaine shrugged because this wasn't her problem. She only wanted to protect her friends, family and species from the Keres.

The law helped her do that.

The Keres tried to reach across the table but she couldn't and Elaine was so glad about that.

"Please. This isn't right. I pay for those goods, I might not have returned them when asked but that was because this isn't right. The Keres are victimised at every single turn,"

As much as Elaine wanted to leave because she had her confession, she actually wanted to listen for just a moment longer. Because emotionally she couldn't understand where the hell this whacko alien was coming from, but at an intelligence and rational level, the alien made a good point.

"Your species signed the Treaty of Defeat. They could have chosen not to. If you're mad at the laws you are subject to then be mad at your Creator or whatever weird name you have for him,"

The Keres shook her head. "You lie and you don't know your own history. The Keres were forced to sign those documents or your humanity was going to nuke our entire Empire and ten planets of your own,"

Elaine laughed. This alien needed to be locked away desperately. She was a psycho.

"Our Creator could live with the sacrifice and defeat of our species but we wouldn't allow your Rex to annihilate hundreds of billions of his own people and he knew that,"

Elaine just laughed because this alien was just making up so many excuses for her criminal actions, but she couldn't help but feel like she wasn't lying.

Her father had served in the War and even though he had come back a changed man because of the things he had seen, he had been drunk one night and he had mentioned about killing humans.

Elaine had always dismissed the memory but what if her father wasn't wrong?

She just looked at the foul alien scum and shook her head. This wasn't right and this was just another manipulation that the Keres was using on her.

She had her confession and thankfully this alien was going to be locked away for a very, very long time.

Elaine got up to leave but the Keres spoke to her. "I feel sorry for humanity because your Rex pumps out so much hate, propaganda and lies that even you cannot tell the difference between right and wrong. Oh, wow humanity has lost its way,"

Elaine just left the scum in the room because she didn't have time for any more lies.

But deep, deep down Elaine had to admit that the Keres might not be wrong after all.

***

After a great, wonderful and sensational day of working another ten more cases involving the disgusting Keres, Elaine sat back on her delightful chair and sterile white cubicle that stopped her from seeing the other workers that had their own white cubicles and Elaine had to admit today had been weird.

Her bosses had said how great, ruthless and cunning she was because she had managed to get a confession from each of the Keres criminals, but the words of the first Keres had only grown in her mind with each case.

She had interrogated and charged all ten of the other Keres today and if she really had to admit it, they were all for silly petty crimes that humans couldn't actually get charged for.

Like her last case was charging a Keres for "assaulting" a human when all that had actually happened was the Keres had been tripped over by an elderly woman and the male Keres had fallen on top of a female teenager.

The Keres had been arrested and Elaine had charged him for a hundred years to be served on a mining world by making him do forced labour.

And as the wonderful smells of mint, lavender and caramel formed in the air, Elaine couldn't help but wonder if this was right in the slightest. And each of the Keres had told her differing stories to how the Keres Empire had come to sign onto the Treaty of Defeat and none of them matched the Rex's version.

Was it possible that Elaine was lied to?

Elaine had no idea and if she was thinking about this from a legal and historical viewpoint (because she had studied history briefly before the Rex outlawed history) she had to admit it was very, very possible.

But that was a problem for another day, Elaine was one woman in one law firm on one planet of the Imperium. She couldn't do anything about it and if she didn't convict Keres people then she couldn't get paid.

Yet she couldn't deny that it wasn't fair so

maybe, just maybe one day she could help change all of that but it was a very, very long way away and Elaine had a large amount of criminals to deal with first.

So Elaine had to return to the job and caseload she loved with a new sense of injustice that she knew would morph into action at some point and the Keres would be saved.

ENEMY OF HISTORY

Librarian Aria Pinncock had always loved her library with its immense wooden shelves and dark varnish that stretched on for hundreds of miles and the tourists flocked to see the library just for the shelves alone. You couldn't see wooden shelves anywhere else in the Imperium, and Aria really did love the soft blue carpet. It was just such a strange texture that also wasn't found anywhere else in the Imperium.

She stood on the very bottom of the great wooden staircase that went elegantly up towards the second, third and fourth floors of the immense library that she had come to love so much. The staircase was a real beaut with its solid oak railing that were handcrafted on Earth itself with all sorts of designs that the Rex personally approved for the library.

Aria wasn't really sure that she liked it when the tourists said that the staircase was holy or something because the Rex had apparently touched it himself.

But considering just how much propaganda there was in the Imperium, it was impossible to tell.

Aria still loved her job.

The staircase even had a couple of marks, scratches and worn patches where so many great scholars had been working away and going up and down to investigate their latest project.

Aria really had enjoyed her career in academia and she had always liked this library even more. Especially with its rows upon rows of real blue leather-bound hardbacks, as the Head Librarian Aria was always searching for more but most of the books she bought were confiscated by the Rex.

Damn him.

It was always such a rarity to see real print books these days with their soft leather covers, musty smell and cold to the touch that Aria never wanted to leave her library. It was a place of knowledge and she had seen the first-hand impacts of the Rex's great campaign to suppress knowledge.

People talking, muttering and even shouting caught Aria's attention as a large group of white robbed scholars were walking towards the staircase. Aria didn't allow them to worry her for now.

Aria had gone on holiday plenty of times to the other systems without a librarian like herself that prized knowledge beyond all else. So many millions of people died because their medical care was shambolic, all because the Rex had suppressed important medical textbooks because of the so-called evil knowledge inside certain passages.

Apparently the Rex was going to rewrite all the books he confiscated but Aria had never seen such books.

It was why she had been kicked out of academia and she had lost her history job, her fellow professors and best friends were imprisoned for not agreeing to rewrite history books for Rex and she actually had no idea what happened to them. Aria was only saved because a few decades ago her family were rich, powerful and the Rex liked them a great deal.

Aria hadn't spoken to them for decades, she just wanted to keep them safe. When she started learning about history she never ever imagined it would become a crime.

"Excuse me," a man said.

Aria looked at the man and forced herself not to frown at the four white robed men that looked awful in their sterile white cloth robes that meant they were from the Rex's personal university on Earth. These men were probably the most indoctrinated people in the Imperium into the cult of the Rex's lies, deceit and corruption.

She couldn't allow these people to do anything against her, her library or any of the thousands of people on all the floors. She had to protect them.

The sweet aromas of pine, cherry and apples filled Aria's senses leaving the wonderful taste of warm apple pie on her tongue just like how her mother had baked when she was a child. Her mother would have hated what the Rex had done to history.

"Yes, what can I do for you fine gentleman?" Aria asked.

Aria noticed that she couldn't see any of the men's faces. It was like they were shrouded in a form of shadow that wasn't dark nor light.

"We are seeking a book called the Enlighted Bible," one of the men said.

Aria slowly nodded making it seem like she was searching her memories. Of course she knew exactly what book they were referring to, it was her favourite purchase this year, a book confirming the existence of a breakaway democratic republic of humans away from the Rex's control.

That was an amazing find so she couldn't allow these stupid men to find the book and destroy it.

"That book is a danger to the safety of the Imperium," another man said. "That book contains knowledge that has the potential to shake the Imperium to its core and cause a civil war,"

Aria seriously doubted that because she had read the first few pages (more than enough to get her killed) and the book was just describing a life of freedom, learning and pleasure in the solar systems controlled by the Enlightened Republic.

"I do not know of this book," Aria said, knowing she was done for.

Aria looked around in some vain hope of trying

to find an escape path or something but there wasn't one. She knew every single inch of this library and there was no escape. She already had a feeling there were more white robed men on other floors just waiting for her to escape.

And those men would kill her.

"I just wanted to learn about the past, learning is not a crime," Aria said.

The men laughed and the tallest of the men stepped forward and arrested Aria, handcuffing her with holographic cuffs.

"Aria Pinncock you are an Enemy of The True History of Humanity and you are a terrorist trying to spread lies and corruption about the Great Rex," he said.

Aria just laughed as the men led her away and she quickly realised that she had to escape no matter what because these men would interrogate her to find the book.

But once they had the book they would kill her.

***

The awful aromas of burnt petrol, ozone and death filled Aria's senses as she leant against the icy cold black metal wall of the interrogation chamber. She was half expecting something grander considering these people were most probably the top-secret organisation known as the *Erasers*.

But the interrogation chamber was nothing more than a black metal box without a table or chair or very good environmental systems it turned out. It was just all rather uncreative but she supposed that was the point.

She, like everyone else in the Imperium, knew that if someone was picked up by the Erasers then they really were as good as dead and the Erasers on the interrogation ship were in constant communication with the ground force. So sooner or later the book would be found by the ground force and whoever came to interrogate her would kill her.

And it was even worse that the interrogations always happened on a big bulky circular ship that always struck fear in the hearts of humans whenever they saw it. Aria really hated it how she was now on one of those damn ships.

Aria had no idea whatsoever if she had done enough to hide the book. All she actually wanted was to finish reading it, learning about it and developing her knowledge about what the galaxy was really like instead of what the Rex wanted her to believe.

"Do not attack," a female computerised voice said.

Aria stood up perfectly straight as the deafening roar of a faulty teleportation hummed around the chamber.

A moment later a very tall white robed woman appeared, she looked the same as the men but her boots were black and she actually had her hood up.

And Aria couldn't help but feel like she was hearing a strange sound in the background but she couldn't quite identify what it was.

"You are currently listening to psycho-conditioning files making you more likely to tell me the location of the book," the woman said coldly. "You are a terrorist and you will die but how quickly and painfully is down to you,"

Aria just couldn't understand how the hell the Imperium had actually gotten like this, it was just impossible to imagine how an Imperium that loved, treasured and worshipped learning and history had gone so backwards so quickly.

"I will not allow you to destroy knowledge," Aria said.

The woman laughed. "Knowledge is nothing more than a weapon. Whoever controls knowledge controls people. The Rex controls knowledge so he controls every human in the Imperium and he basically controls the Keres too,"

Aria bit her lip at the sheer mention of alien Keres. A poor innocent alien race with beautiful magic that the Rex had decided were a threat so he bullied them into a war and submission and crippled a peaceful race.

Aria hated it when she had learnt the truth about the Keres, but sadly that history book had been burnt by a "friend" of hers. She was so glad she pushed him through an airlock, by accident of course.

"I will ask you three times a simple question and if you do not tell me after the third question I will kill you using crippling pain. Where is the book?"

Aria looked around. She had barely any time to free herself and she really had no intention of dying today.

Her former husband that died a few years ago fighting the Keres in the futile war would have wanted her to go out and find love again. And her mother would want her to protect history.

"Okay then you are refusing to answer me," the woman said.

Aria focused on the seams of the interrogation chamber but the damn workmanship was so fine that the entire chamber seemed to be moulded from a single sheet of steel.

There were no weak points.

Aria stood up and started tapping the walls.

"You will not find anything. Where is the book?"

Aria frowned. She really was running out of time to escape and then she realised that she was a history professor first and foremost regardless of whatever the Rex said.

Two hundred years ago when the Erasers were first founded, Aria read an article and interview written by an escapee before she was brutally burnt alive but she wrote that no one watched the interrogations and the only people who could escape were the interrogators.

That was what Aria needed to focus on. And because the woman had teleported in, she had to have a teleporter on her.

Aria just looked at the woman and smiled. The woman seemed to shudder.

Aria went over to the woman and placed her hands around her neck. The woman didn't seem to react but Aria pulled her hood down. Revealing the woman had a cybernetic eye so someone was watching her.

"You read the interview too then," the woman said. "I was like you once but no one escapes this place,"

Aria spat at the woman as she realised the so-called escapee was just a trap to lure idiots like her to their deaths. But her plan was still going to work.

Aria punched the woman, smashing her eye so no one else was watching them and she knew she only had moments left before someone checked on her.

Aria quickly changed clothes with the woman and made sure that the hood was up on her and the woman interrogator was dressed in her clothes.

A moment later three large black armoured humans appeared and Aria just looked at them with such a fierce aura of authority that the men actually bowed at her.

Aria really loved the technology that shrouded her face from the men's glare.

"She is dead. Let us leave," Aria said.

The men nodded and the deafening roar of a faulty teleportation filled the air and Aria just smiled as she teleported away and now she just needed to escape this ship before her deception was found out.

***

A few hours later, Aria crawled up into a small little ball inside the large(ish) bright white pod of a space shuttle that she had stolen from the Eraser Ship. She had tried to disable the tracker, the autopilot and all the rest of the annoying things that the Imperium installed on their shuttles and ships to make sure people like her didn't steal them, but she wasn't sure.

She had been flying for about an hour and the circular Eraser Ship didn't seem to be tracking her or anything so it seemed to be okay for now. Aria just wanted to get away from the Imperium, the Rex's forces and actually just wanted freedom.

The pod shuttle was thankfully simple and it wasn't too hard to figure out it worked with only a few bright white holograms forming her commands for her.

She had already worked out how to make the shuttle speed up, slow down and turn a little so hopefully that was everything she really needed to know for the moment. The pod also had some great environmental systems with the sweet senses of apple pie, pecans and oranges filling the air and after being interrogated it was such a relaxing smell.

As Aria watched the pitch darkness of space slowly go past her with bright white stars in the distance and a handful of planets from her home system going past, Aria just smiled because she might have been a criminal now and an enemy of the Rex's true history, but she was free.

Freedom was a myth in the Imperium and now Aria could finally go out and seek the amazing Enlightened Republic. She would live there, get to taste their way of life and most importantly she would get to learn what history was actually like.

Because the Rex could always try to take the girl out of history, but it was impossible to take the history out of the girl. And that was why she loved being an enemy of history.

WATCHING THE WRECK

When I, Mila Scott, was younger I actually loved going into the cold, darkness of space with my brothers and sisters flying about in our junker of a space shuttle. An awful little pod-like object that I was always scared of it falling apart, that was exactly how old it was. Me and my sisters and brothers saw some wonderful things in the Imperium, massive stars, circular battleships and little bright white pods that tried to kill us once or twice.

Those really were the days of our youth that I absolutely loved. Then as we all grew older, a little fatter and not a lot wiser, we all went our separate and rather different ways.

My three brothers they joined the Imperial Army and all died during the stupid war with the peaceful aliens known as the Keres, all because our stupid leader the Rex was scared of their magic. They all died.

My sisters went to study medicine on Earth, a so-called great honour but because both of them were certainly daughters of our mother, they questioned way too much and I think the Erasers killed them so others wouldn't question the Rex's version of events.

That's the silly galaxy we live in.

And as for little old me, well I was stupid enough to study history and become a history graduate, I even have a PhD in Early Imperium Studies and the Rex hates that subject.

That's why I'm sitting pretty at my bright white metal desk inside my even whiter cubicle with its awfully smooth walls that I hate, and I'm having to stare at a little holographic computer screen.

Thankfully, there's a small red dot flashing at the very, very edge of my computer screen but until it gets closer towards the centre of my screen, I really don't want to do anything about it.

Personally I just want to add some holo-art of something to the perfectly smooth walls but I cannot. Apparently that would endanger my life, it's rubbish of course but I always like to see their excuses for controlling every single aspect of my life.

The cubicle itself isn't so bad I suppose, there's a brand-new small single bed that is rather comfortable, it just sits behind me during the day and it doubles as a sofa and dining table. The people in charge here don't exactly give you much.

Granted, I hate its soft blue sheets because I could have sworn the bosses here coat the material in a waxy substance that annoys me when I go to sleep. I also flat out the little food shoot, that really is nothing more than a metal pipe that drops food into my cubicle.

I mean I am no dog, cat or animal so why can't I just get given food like every other normal person in the Imperium. Normally food is just shipped to entire planets from Farming Worlds but clearly that might not happen here.

And the smell is just the worse at feeding time, because the pipe connects directly outside the cubicle gets filled with the disgusting senses of burnt ozone, petrol and raw meat. It flat out isn't a nice place, I hate it.

"Three minutes until Exercise Time," a loud computerised voice said.

Oh yes, if you can believe it. The bosses here actually give us very set exercise time, it's basically the only ten minutes we're allowed to leave these cubicles each day. And that's why I'm so excited about when I can finally leave this form of prison.

Officially, when the Rex decided to outlaw history (because it was the only thing that could challenge his lies), he arrested, killed and captured all the history professionals in the Imperium. I was one of the "Lucky" few that got to enlist in the army and now I am stuck on this awful military moon just watching the border between the Imperium and the dying Keres Empire.

In other words, I get to stare at pitch darkness all

day.

And my mother said studying history was a brilliant idea.

The wonderful sounds of my friends (my other inmates) laughing, talking and discussing what they're found on their computer screens is loud enough to get through the thick white walls, and I'm so looking forward to seeing them.

Even ten minutes with them is a wonderful distraction to the mind numbing pain of this prison.

I get up and past my bed where the wall should dissolve and I should be able to go outside.

"Not for you. You have an object on your screen. You must sort it out first before going for your exercise time, no extra time will be given," the computerised voice said.

I wanted to smash my fists into a wall or something. How dare this stupid voice and my bosses deduct my exercise time from me just because of some dumb red spot.

I went back over to my computer screen and tapped my fingers on the spot.

I read the output as the tapping always gave me a light reading and scan of whatever the object was. It was certainly Imperium in nature, I would recognise the black circular design anywhere.

But the materials were all wrong, and my knowledge of history and my wonderful relationship with a boy studying Military History (he was one that got a bullet in the head by the Rex), I knew these materials haven't been used in two thousand years to build Imperium ships.

I zoom in even more because I just couldn't understand this, this ship is coming in the direction of the Keres Empire and yet this is an Imperium vessel.

The Keres Empire have always, always been peaceful, magical and great aliens that truly respect humanity, well unlike humanity determined to slaughter them, and even the most extreme elements of Keres society (that only came about because of the war) would never keep an Imperium vessel and then return it later on.

That was a very human thing to do.

"Computer," I said, "I need access to the others,"

"Access denied. You are a Level 5 Operative, you do not need lessers to help you," the voice said.

Damn it. I seriously hated my bosses, and part of the problem was that I actually was that good unfortunately so the bosses trusted me. I had sadly stopped a number of smuggling ships trying to bring Keres refugees into Imperial space so they could get food, medical supplies and clean water for their people.

All things that the Imperium had stolen from them after the war.

I zoomed in and really focused on the circular ship and I started to scan it deeply. I had to know what was going on here.

The ship had no power, no engines, no weapon systems. All of it had been taken out and that actually was a rather Keres thing to do because it helped them to maintain the peace, but there were also no bodies.

Typically, and the Rex would never admit this, the Keres always used their magic to knock out the human attackers so they could enter a peaceful sleep and then the Keres would return the attackers to the Imperium.

That was partly why they lost the war. Their commitment to peace was amazing if not their downfall.

Then a single reading popped up and I just smiled. It turned out there was a single corpse on the ship and it proved everything I ever wanted to do about the ship.

There was an Imperial corpse on the ship, meaning a murder had taken place and if there was one thing my bosses hated it was a dead body.

Now I just needed to play it to my advantage.

I just hoped that the computer and my bosses had forgotten how me and my friends were all excellent coders and we could easily manipulate a hologram system to scan for whatever we want. It was amazing the skills you could pick up.

I could easily do this work on my own but I just wanted to see my friends and most importantly I wanted to see if there was a chance of escape.

I didn't want to be stuck on this damn moon

anymore.

"Computer, I need access to the others now. There's a dead human on that ship and if killers are onboard then we have to know before it reaches Imperial Space," I said, hoping beyond hope it would work.

There was a long pause.

"Granted. Doors will open now and everyone will meet in the Command Centre," the voice said.

I weakly smiled, not only because I was going to get a chance to see my friends but also because the Command Centre was where our captors or "bosses" were. And I had always known some of my friends wanted their freedom.

Maybe this was the time to fight for our freedom too.

***

Now granted, I have never been to the command centre before but I would have imagined it was a little more high-tech than this junk.

I was standing in nothing more than a large dirty white cubicle about four times bigger than my own cubicle, so it was still rather small. There were barely any holograms, and the only white holograms there were were about the weather, not something I'm very interested in knowing about on a moon.

There was a small porthole that was just showed how the bright orange rock of the moon stretched on endlessly with craters, unexploded bombs and our cubicles punctuating the orange rock.

It was not pretty.

Thankfully, there was a huge holographic table in the middle of the command centre showing a large flickering depiction of the black circular wreck I had found earlier.

And all my friends were here, which was amazing.

There were only five other people here out of ten, so I was a little worried about where they were but I didn't mind.

My best friend in the entire galaxy, Paula was standing next to me in her normal pink jeans, hoody and boots. She was more than ready to work.

"This is a wreck from two centuries before the Keres War," a man called Andy said, sporting a very dirty jacket that looked like it was about to fall apart at any moment.

"But how did it end up behind Keres lines?" Paula said.

"Well I don't know what we can say without getting killed," James said, a very short man.

I smiled because that was the truth of it. We could all easily solve this mystery if we were allowed to discuss history but of course that would only get us all killed.

And I really didn't like the gentle humming of the command centre, almost like our bosses were preparing to gas us all at a moment's notice.

"Wait, so we all know if we don't solve this

mystery with the wreck, we don't get fed tonight but could this be an opportunity?" I said.

Well, if our bosses were going to gas us anyway, I at least wanted to know if the others wanted freedom.

"From what I remember, the Imperium has always used the other basic communication network," Andy said.

I nodded as I swiped the holographic table a few times and tried to establish a connection with the wreck. Then I remembered how it didn't have any power.

The holographic table flashed and a small warning hologram came up. It was saying the scan had just been scanned by a magical sign.

"There's Keres on that ship," Paula said, failing to show her excitement.

I didn't want to comment as I heard the command centre humming even louder and the others were starting to show their own concern at the sound.

If I wanted to make sure me and my friends survived this then I had to be very careful here. The problem was that this command centre was set to kill us so we could never escape and pass on our historical knowledge to anyone else. Including the Keres.

Another problem was that the Keres were sending a wreckage towards us and I don't know why.

And to make things even worse, my friends were building their assumption on the Keres were here to save us. What if they weren't?

But as the humming of the command centre reached a deafening level, I just knew I couldn't wait around for answers. We needed to escape now, ideally find our bosses and kill them.

"Cannons activating," a computerised voice said.

"Damn it," I said.

Our bosses were preparing to destroy the wreckage so the Keres died and we couldn't escape. Damn them. Damn the Rex. Damn the Imperium.

As one me and my friends all started typing on the holographic table and tried to access the moon's central mainframe so we could access all computer systems on the moon.

"I did it," Paula said.

I moved round to her set of holograms. I was the best coder amongst all of us so I took control.

Our bosses were fighting us and trying to force us out but they were thinking I was going after the cannons.

I wasn't.

Our bosses kicked out everyone else from the system but I was here logged in. I was going after the gas and environmental systems that would ultimately kill us.

I found them. Then I programmed the environmental systems to pump the toxic gas into the chamber where my bosses were.

The system complied and the loud deafening

screams of my bosses echoed around the command centre as I played the audio from their chamber beneath us.

My friends laughed, hugged each other and I loved their sheer happiness but I had to save the Keres. The cannons were still being activated and then the results of a much better scan came in that Andy had started running in secret.

There were thousands of Keres refugees on the ship that had been using their magic to shield themselves from scanning. And in fact the entire wreckage wasn't Imperial in nature, it was a beautifully, bejewelled stunning Keres battleship.

I had to save those innocent people.

I found the cannons. They were about to fire.

I hit the kill code but it didn't work.

I tried changing the target.

It didn't work.

So I tried to kill the power.

All the power on the moon deactivated and everything went perfectly silent and it was only in the sheer deadly silence of the moon that I realised just how much background noise I had tuned out since I got here.

But that included the environmental systems were off too.

And it wasn't like I could reactivate the power because the cannon commands were still in the computer system waiting to be carried out the moment there was power again.

I just looked at all my amazing friends, Paula, Andy and the rest. They all looked so shocked but they were smiling.

Not because they were happy about dying on some moon that they hated, but because they were going to sacrifice themselves so innocent people could live.

I was damn proud of them.

My lungs jerked as I tried to breathe in air that wasn't there and then my lungs burnt painfully as they screamed out for air. Air that was never coming for them.

I was about to shut my eyes and allow the darkness of death to claim me when I felt a warm magical energy wrap around me and my vision was blinded by a beautiful golden light.

***

When I opened my eyes again, I couldn't exactly understand why I was laying down on something hard, light blue and oddly warm but it was nice, so much nicer than anything human I had ever felt.

I pushed myself and allowed my legs to dangle over the edge, and I was pleased that it was a sort of medical table that I had been sitting on. It looked like it was made from a yellow sort of plastic but the Keres were always masters of technology and making things. This was probably a material I had never thought of before.

The medical chamber itself was stylish and like a

massive pod with beautiful baby blue walls with the artist's brush marks swirling, twirling and whirling around each other. It was so beautiful to look at and even the jewelled ceiling with diamonds, rubies and stranger, more alien gems was simply stunning.

The quiet humming, laughing and talking of my best friends gave me such relief. At least they were alive, well and seemingly very happy so at least I didn't get everyone killed, and it was only now that I was realising exactly what we had done.

We had saved so many innocent people from dying a painful death, we had finally escaped our bosses and that damn moon so now the Imperium could no longer watch their precious border with the Keres Empire in case an invasion even happened.

But it wouldn't and I was okay with that because me and my friends were free.

The sweet smells of oranges, jasmine and lemons filled the air as a section of the wall dissolved and in came a very thin and male Keres. He was humanoid in shape and features but he was much tall, almost dangerously thin and he certainly looked a lot more regal than humans ever could.

"Thank you," the male Keres said bowing elegantly.

"No, thank you for saving us. You can drop us off wherever, me and my friends don't want to burden you,"

The Keres laughed so beautifully that it was like listening to a melody. "Now it seems you are being silly because your crew have already accepted an offer of employment, and I hope you will accept it too. Live with us and join us and become one of us or yes, we will drop you off whenever you desire,"

If this person wasn't Keres then I naturally would have denied it because this was a very dangerous offer. But I am a history professor and Doctor of History, I know that the Keres are deeply caring, supportive and protective people and they will always see me and my crew as one of them.

If we live with the Keres then we will never be in danger from them, they will live freely and we can actually experience joy once more. And I want that so badly.

"I accept," I said bowing to the Keres as that was their equivalent of a handshake.

"Excellent, your friends are in the dining chamber playing, I think you call it, carks?"

Because he was being so nice to me, my friends and he had offered us freedom and joy after a lifetime of pain, I didn't care to correct him. But as I left the medical chamber, I was looking forward to playing *cards*, starting my new life and finally start watching the Imperium from the other side and I have to admit it really will be like watching a wreckage that would never enslave me again.

Because I wouldn't let it.

AN ENLIGHTENED BAR

Former Imperial Army soldier Henry Dixon sat on an icy cold little metal bar stool that was surprisingly comfortable given how it was nothing but cold metal touching his rear. The bar he sat at had warming touches of oranges, reds and yellows in a stylish design along its immense wooden counter, but it still felt strange.

The so-called Enlightening Bar was the only pub on the entire circular space station and as much as Henry had wanted to avoid it like the plague, because its name sounded like a cult, after two weeks of living on the space station he just couldn't resist anymore.

The bar was a lot nicer than he was expecting, but given how he had spent his youth in the swampy wastelands of planets he could only remember killing innocent aliens for the Imperium, anything was better than in comparison.

And the sheer silence of the bar was so, so nice. Henry really loved the silence, or at least it was silent compared to the damn swamps.

It might have been three o'clock in the afternoon but Henry was still impressed there were over twenty people in long sweeping gowns, jeans and holo-clothes that sadly failed from time to time revealing the horror of their owner's bodies below.

Whilst all those people were tucked around the bar's large grey tables that helped to give the bar a little bit of an industrial feel, Henry couldn't take his eyes off one very cute woman behind the bar counter. She was so beautiful with her smooth cheeks, long sexy legs and her bar uniform was certainly too small.

That wasn't a problem though. Henry seriously didn't mind.

The rest of the bar was covered in dark tones of browns, blacks and greys that might have made Henry want to be clear of this place come the evening crowd but it made everyone focus on the warming, welcoming, inviting bar counter so he didn't want to leave yet.

Not at least until he could talk to the beautiful woman behind it some more.

The woman started mixing a cocktail and the air was filled with stunning hints of strawberry, raspberry and mint syrup that was so outstanding that Henry could actually taste the cocktail form on his tongue.

Then the woman poured herself the drink and leant against the bar opposite Henry.

He checked his teeth with his tongue in case he

had a bit of food stuck in his teeth and when he found nothing, he just couldn't understand why she was looking at him.

Then he realised she was actually grinning at him.

"What did you do in your old life?" she asked.

Henry weakly smiled.

Ever since he had come to the Enlightened Republic over two weeks ago, to escape the evil, murderous, tyrannical Imperium, he had been surprised to meet so many other people that just wanted a life of freedom, justice and democracy. Something humanity could only find in the Republic.

"I was a former Imperial Army soldier," Henry said and the entire bar went silent.

He looked over to the other patrons and they were just staring at him like he was some kind of monster that could kill them at any moment.

Even the ever-present hum, pop and vibrating of the space station's engines seem to stop at his revelation.

Henry looked back at the woman. "I thought it was normal to flee here when you realised the Rex was a murderous bastard that only saw humanity as cattle to control and kill?"

The woman extended her hand. "It is and I'm glad you're here. My name is Brielle but my friends call me Brie,"

Henry shook her hand hard and was surprised that she shook his hand so hard he wondered when it was going to break.

"What were you in your former life?" Henry asked.

"This will make you laugh. I was a former Imperial Assassin for the Rex himself," Brie said grinning.

Henry's mouth just dropped. There was literally nothing he could ever say to that. The Imperial Assassins were some of the most indoctrinated, controlled and loyal to the Rex, it was impossible for her to escape the Rex's control.

He had no idea if she was a threat or not to the Republic but he was going to have to watch her.

The other patrons of the bar and the tight security network of the republic might not have cared but Henry certainly did. He had worked with Imperial Assassins before and he hated it every single time.

They always killed more and more loyal troops that failed to show enough "worship" to the Rex. The assassins were that crazy.

"I don't follow him anymore you know. I escaped just like you ten years ago and now I am one out of two thousand bars and pubs in the entire Republic providing a social space for the travellers and refugees that need it,"

As much as Henry didn't want to admit it, he did sadly believe her but he just didn't understand the name of the bar.

"Why The Enlightening Bar?" Henry asked.

Again the entire bar went silent and then he

heard everyone getting up, paid for their drinks using their Enlightened Credits and they left. Henry's stomach twisted into a painful knot.

"Did I do something wrong?" he asked.

Brie smiled. "No, you really didn't. It is that the whole Enlightening Bar thing is a secret message used by the Republic to hunt out the curious minds amongst us so they can learn a fundamental truth,"

I went to stand up and leave but my body wasn't responding. I clearly wanted to keep listening and I had to admit I was interested.

Brie came out and sat next to me. "As you know the Enlightened Republic is named so because only the humans that realise what the Rex is doing is wrong come here,"

Henry nodded. That was exactly what he knew and why he was pleased to call himself an Enlightened.

"But there is a secondary truth that needs to be learnt for the sake of humanity. The Rex and the Imperium have rejected this truth and most of the Republic have too,"

Henry really didn't like where this was going. All he had wanted was a nice social space to meet people, grab a drink and maybe have sex with Brie later.

That was it.

"What truth could possibly be so important but ultimately rejected by humanity?" Henry asked.

Brie grinned and looked around but they both knew no one else was in the bar.

"There was Gods and Goddesses in this galaxy and the Keres are not our foes," Brie said.

Henry just laughed. He knew that the Keres were innocent humanoid aliens that just wanted to live in peace and use their magic for good but then the Rex had launched an obliterating war against them.

He wasn't sure what happened to the Keres now, he knew they were dying out as a species but Henry couldn't understand why that truth would be a revelation to humans.

"There was things in this galaxy. Humans do not understand," Brie said, "and if you want I can show you the truth about what the Keres are doing both for and against us and then you can decide what you want to do with the information,"

Henry just nodded. Brie had to be crazy or something.

"Okay show me this truth," Henry said.

Brie frowned and she started to mix up a bright red, purple and orange sparkling drinks in a whiskey crystal glass. The tendrils of colour swirled and whirled around each other like it was alive and then Brief handed it to Henry.

"Drink,"

Henry smelt it enjoying the sweet aromas of pineapples, mint and freshly cut grass. Then he drank it.

He felt the bar fall away from him.

A few moments later he realised that he was still

sitting in the bar in the exact same place as before with the grey metal tables behind him, the bar counter with its warming colours and there were plenty of bottles of alcohol behind the bar.

But everything looked slightly blurry almost like Henry was so drunk he couldn't see clearly.

Even the sounds of the bar were weird because all Henry could hear was the calming sound of the ocean roaring away in his ears, and the smell of sea salt invaded in his senses.

He clearly wasn't in the bar anymore. He had no idea where he was.

Henry went to get up and he stumbled off the seat and standing in front of him was a female Keres. A beautiful alien woman that looked like a human female just a lot thinner with sharper, pointier features and long pointy ears.

"You came a long way for no reason," she said. Her voice sharp, cutting and struggling to make certain letters.

"I came to learn the truth," Henry said but his voice was nothing more than an echo cutting through the roar of the sea.

"Humanity is doomed," the woman said. "I tried to warn your race against the war. I tried to warn them against Ultraspace. I tried so damn hard to help you guys but the Gods and Goddesses of death are coming for you,"

Henry stared at her. He had no idea why she would try to warn humanity against using the

Ultraspace network, the brilliant interdimensional tunnel network that allowed humans to travel from one side of the galaxy to another in a matter of months, not centuries.

"You pushed my race to extinction," the Keres said. "There are those of us that are now infuriated by humanity for the last time. We are hunting down the Shards of the Geneitor, we will find him and we will unleash him on the galaxy once more so he can finally wipe out humanity once and for all,"

Henry took a step forward, reached out for her but his fingers simply fell through her and then the Keres started laughing.

The laughter rang like a bomb in his ears. His ears bleed and then Henry fell his entire world fell away from him.

***

"Please wake up," Brie said.

A few hours later, Henry found himself laying his head on the bar stool with the loud roar of hip-hop and pop music playing for the evening crowd. There were tons of people in shirts, jeans and holo-clothes dancing about.

The light was a lot darker now but Henry was so glad to see Brie's beautiful face looking at him full of concern. He had never had that before.

"So the Keres are hunting down their Dark Gods," Henry said.

When he was in the military he had done a lot of

work hunting down the Keres, destroying their culture and burning down their books and art, he was just following orders but even then he knew it was wrong. He knew the Keres were peaceful but that never mattered to the Rex.

"Only some of us are hunting them down," a male voice said behind him.

Henry got up off the bar stool and was surprised to see that everyone had stopped dancing, singing and laughing. Everyone was focused on him and actually now he really looked at them, some of them had extremely thin bodies, pointed features and pointed ears.

There were humans and Keres in this bar.

Henry just looked at Brie. "What is this place truly?"

Brie laughed. "There are Enlightening Bars all over the Republic and they're designed for a simple truth and purpose. The leaders of the Republic need humans that can work with the Keres that want to help humanity, fighting against the Dark Keres. The aliens interested in bringing around the End of Days with their resurrection of their Dark Gods,"

A male Keres took Henry by the hand. "If the Dark Keres find all five Gods and then resurrect Geneitor then it is the end of everything. The end of all life in the galaxy,"

Henry couldn't smile, couldn't frown, couldn't do anything. All he could do was just focus on the fierce sense of duty he had felt when the Rex had first conscripted him all those decades ago. He was a young man and he so badly wanted to protect all the innocent humans in the Imperium.

But now he just wanted to protect every single living thing in the galaxy, human or not, he just had to protect them.

Henry smiled at Brie. "Will I get to work with you? And is that why you left the Rex?"

Brie nodded. "During the Human-Keres war, I was going to assassinate a daughter of the Keres Creator called Ithana. She was a servant of the Light Gods and Goddesses and she showed me what was coming. I knew the Rex was too stupid for this but I wanted to protect humanity,"

Henry nodded. He would have done the exact same.

"I travelled to the Enlightened Republic so I could protect humans and Keres alike. And yes if you join us you will be working very *closely* with me,"

Henry nodded and smiled like a little schoolboy. Maybe this could be a great social space for him where he could drink and have sex too. That really would be a perfect life.

"What do I need to do?" Henry asked grinning.

Everyone grabbed and hugged and kissed Henry as the entire bar roared back to life happy to have a brand-new recruit, and as the night continued and the night ended up in Brie's bed, Henry just couldn't believe how excited he was for the future.

A future that might be dark but he certainly wouldn't be alone with a beautiful woman by his side.

IN DEFENCE OF FREEDOM

This was the hour I died.

You see when I was a child, maybe two or three years old, my mother and father sacrificed their lives to smuggle me from the dark tyranny of the Imperium to a place called the Enlightened Republic. I never knew my mother or father, not really anyway, I sometimes have weird images appear in my head of them smiling, kissing my head and the three of us just laughing together.

I knew they really, really loved me.

So as I stood in the brand-new clinically white spherical bridge of my white circular warship, The Hammer of Freedom, I was really hopeful they would be proud of me because I was helping to defend the place they died trying to get me to.

The bridge I had to admit was strange to be in after training for so long. I had always loved the smooth angelic designs of the bridge with its curved walls, bright white walls and flooring that helped to make the bridge feel like daytime even though we were in space and I did like the metal grey throne that I could sit on.

I never did sit on it really. My command throne was just so icy cold and whenever I did sit on it, it just made the situation too real and it reminded me that too many lives depended on my actions.

If I ever failed in my duties to the Enlightened Republic then so many billions of lives were as good as dead. That was a hell of a burden to carry around.

Even the wonderful taste of creamy apple pie clinging to the air wasn't enough to relax me because I knew an attack could happen at any moment. But that apple pie with hints of caramel, ice cream and sweet bitter apples was just sensational.

There were twenty other men and women in the bridge with me and they were all as amazing as each other. I know the whole myth around captain-don't-have-favourites but right now it truly isn't a myth. I loved them all.

My first mate Piper was standing closest to me as she finished running a scan of the nearby area and she was analysing the results like they were the difference between life and death.

Maybe they were.

The entire crew was doing something and I admired that. I had served on warships before and I seriously hated how some crews were lazy when at any moment the Imperium could attack to enslave us.

I had lost way too many friends like that, but at least my crew weren't like that.

They were all so helpful, kind and supportive as they walked around the bridge in their clinically white uniform with a golden pin badge of an angel over their chest symbolising how the Republic was always about freedom, choice and justice.

Nothing like the evil Imperium was. That was all about control, death and murder. The Imperium and their cold leader the Rex were some of the most monstrous people I had ever met.

At least I was safe here away from the evil Imperium as the warship just floated peacefully in space waiting for danger to find us. There weren't any planets nearby, the stars were cold and distant and I couldn't help but wonder why this position needed to be defended.

But apparently according to Supreme General Abbie, this was one of the most important positions to defend in the entire Republic. And I always did what she told me.

"Enemy contacts incoming," Piper said way too calmly for my liking.

"Report," I said, really wanting this to be a joke.

Piper tapped on the massive floor-to-ceiling windows that covered two sides of the bridge and it zoomed in on three incoming circular warships sending out Imperial signals.

"Prepare for battle but don't fire until I give the command," I said.

Everyone nodded and Piper relayed the orders to

the rest of my fleet, another three warships, and my heart leapt to my chest.

The Imperial warships were shiny, brand-new and there wasn't even a single dent in the cold black exterior of the incoming balls of death.

They probably had the best weapons and I knew if they got past us then they could easily jump into Ultraspace and attack the heart of the Republic.

As much as I hated the Ultraspace tunnel network at times because every so often you needed to enter three or four different tunnel networks to get to your destination. Sometimes the Ultraspace network was the only thing protecting the Republic.

Otherwise it would be way too easy for the Imperium to launch their battlefleet into the heart of the Republic and enslave millions.

"Captain, they're haloing us," Piper said.

I looked at her smooth beautiful face and nodded so she would put them through.

No visuals came up but all I was heard the damp heavy breathing of a man before he started talking.

"Captain Thomas Crane you are a good man and we need your help getting into the Republic. We are refugees seeking protection against the Imperium and you need to let us through," the man said.

"Considering I can't even see you that's a firm no. I like to see who I'm talking to," I said knowing this had to be a trap.

The man laughed and Piper took a step closer to me as did a tall man called Bob that I hadn't had a chance to talk to too much.

A moment later a very overweight man appeared in holographic form on the window and I smiled at him knowing that my background was blurred.

"I know you are not a refugee ship," I said. "Your weapons are too new, your ships are too good and you are fools for thinking the Republic would allow such threats into their space,"

The man cocked his head. "I thought the Republic were welcoming,"

"We welcome everyone trying to escape the Imperium but I do not welcome brand-new warships with powerful weapons into our space,"

My bridge went silent and other crew members came closer to me as others stepped away to do their job.

The overweight man grinned at me. "I did tell the Rex this was a stupid idea so I will be frank. My ship is armed with nuclear warheads as are the two warships next to me that are filled with over ten million people wanting to get into the Republic,"

My stomach twisted.

"We collected these people as they tried to flee so the deal is you let me and my forces into the Republic or we kill ten million people. Their blood will be on your hands. I'll give you one minute to decide. If you don't pick up they die,"

Before I could say anything the idiot hung up and I just looked at my crew as they frowned at me. Their eyes were wide and I was almost disappointed that they didn't look like they had any ideas.

I shook my head at them. "It's an impossible choice. If we don't allow them into the Republic then the innocent people die. If you allow them into the Republic then they could kill tens upon tens of millions,"

"It should be a logical choice," Piper said.

"Then why does it feel so hard?" I asked.

My entire crew looked at me and weakly smiled. "Because you're a good man,"

I wasn't so sure about that, I did some questionable things in the Republic Army a few years ago but I got the point.

"What do you need from us?" they asked.

And all I knew was that I absolutely had to try and save these ten million people that were perfectly innocent onboard those warships.

I had to protect the Republic, save the people and protect my crew at the same time. Surely it couldn't be that hard.

"Those nukes onboard the warships, they would have to be detonated remotely right?" I asked.

A young man called Frank came up to the front of the crew and smiled at me. He was a great engineer from what the others had said, it was just a shame this was the first time we were talking.

"Correct sir. Imperial Protocol is to only allow the lead vessel access to the nukes,"

"He's calling again," Piper said.

I nodded and a moment later the fat overweight man reappeared.

"I presume you won't want to save these ten million people but when me and my father went out hunting for scummy poor people when I was a kid. I used to get great joy out of watching the poor scumbags trying to escape my traps. I'll be watching and please, give me a good show before I kill you all,"

He cut the line and I did a quick scan to make sure he wasn't watching us by hacking into our systems. He hadn't thankfully.

"We need to call for reinforcements," a woman said.

I shook my head. "Negative, we need to find a solution. Carry on Frank,"

Frank nodded. "The nukes can only be controlled *and* deactivated from the lead vessel but everything operates on a very sophisticated signal,"

I pointed to the three Imperial warships. "Can you hack into that signal setup and deactivate the nukes from here?"

Frank came to stand next to me and folded his arms. "Negative. I know Republic tech is based on Imperial ones but we use completely different tech setups and I'm not skilled enough to work out the differences,"

I nodded. It was annoying but I understood. I just wanted to protect those innocent people. Then I realised there might have been another way.

I was about to ask about contacting Frank's old boss to see if she could talk him through it but I hated what Piper said next.

"Enemy forces incoming," Piper said.

I double-tapped the window and the ship's computer systems zoomed in the Imperial vessels. They were heading full steam towards us within five minutes they would be within firing range.

We all had to come up with a solution right now.

"I need to do something," I said trying to remember anything at all about my training or records or similar accounts that I've read over the decades.

Nothing. I didn't have a clue.

Then I wondered what if I made an impossible bargain that would kill me but save everything I loved.

I looked at Frank. "Could you give me a device that would scan a ship's signals and hijack any nuke-relate ones?"

Frank nodded. "I can do that. You would be closer to the source so it would be easier than doing it remotely. Why?"

I just looked at the incoming enemy warships and smiled. "Because I'm going on board that warship, I'm going to die and I'm going to save everyone,"

My entire crew shook their heads and the deadly silence told me everything I needed to know.

We all knew it was the only way.

***

I was somewhat surprised how easy it was to get the Imperial commander to allow me to go onto the bridge, they didn't even search me because apparently the Republic was so pathetic it wasn't a threat, but now my stomach was twisting into an agonising knot as I realised what was going to happen next.

I stood in the middle of a large boxroom of a bridge with awful cream-coloured walls, a horrible smell of bleach and the overweight male commander just stunk of tobacco.

Unlike before on the hologram I could now see the commander was ugly with blackened teeth, an immense beer gut that came from drinking too much instead of doing your duty and his black hair looked like a bird's nest more than anything else.

I was the only other person on the bridge besides the commander and I so badly wanted to kill him as he wore his ugly black Imperial Army uniform, but instead I just smiled and I pressed the button on a small black device that started searching for nuke signals.

The realisation was finally hitting me that I was going to die. I didn't want to die, I hated dying, I almost felt like I was betraying the sacrifice of my parents. But all I wanted, needed to do with my life was protect the Republic, the innocent and my crew.

If dying meant doing that then I was happy to do it.

"What's the plan now then?" the Commander

asked.

"There isn't one or to be honest, I'm hoping you'll be talking long enough for me to escape and kill you," I said lying.

The Commander nodded like he believed me but then he frowned as a red light on his wrist started flashing.

"Lying to me isn't good. I know you're searching for nuclear signals and, what? You wanted to hijack the signals and deactivate them?"

I didn't dare react. He could have been fishing and I was not going to confirm his crazy ideas about me.

"Shame," he said, "I was hoping for a good show but you see the nukes aren't all tied together and I don't control them,"

I just looked at him.

"This is a suicide mission for both of us it seems," the commander said. "The Rex controls the nukes and I failed him too many times so now he wants to kill me, your Republic and the refugees in the two other ships,"

I didn't want to believe this but from everything I've heard from others fleeing the Imperium, the historical documents I'd read and the things I saw when I visited the Imperium twice, I knew he was telling the truth. The Rex really was that crazy.

"I'm sorry," the commander said. "I'm sorry for all of this and now I don't know how to fix this,"

A loud deafening roar echoed overhead and I

presumed that was the sound of the nukes charging up. They were going to explode shortly.

I had to find a way out of this. I had to live. I had to save the innocent people.

"We have to save them," I said. "Don't you Imperial guys have signal blockers?"

The commander shrugged and just stared into space like it was the last thing he might ever see. It probably would be unless he helped me.

But he was useless.

I hadn't focused on the walls or equipment in the boxroom bridge before so I went over to some kind of cuboid thing and pressed some of the switches on it.

A whole bunch of communication channels started to appear, I looked through the call history and found my ship. I dialled.

A moment later Piper's wonderful face appeared.

"Get me Frank now," I said.

Frank's face appeared.

"I need to know how to block signals,"

Frank nodded. "Okay you need to enter the following code very carefully into the Imperial vessel. My old mentor taught me this as a joke and-"

"Don't have time for this," I said.

Then Frank told me exactly what to do about the code. The deafening scream of the nuclear warheads got louder and louder and I typed faster and faster.

I entered the code and then the nukes started

popping.

Then silence.

The communication channel with Frank cut out and the commander just looked at me and grinned.

Then he pulled a gun out.

"Thanks for saving me mate," he said. "But I cannot let you live. There is still hope for me with the Rex. You might have blocked the signals he was sending but I can prove myself useful,"

As he kept preaching his pathetic delusions about how the Rex might forgive him (but if the Rex was prepared to nuke him I doubt it) I accessed the signals and computer systems that kept the nukes linked together and a simple diagram appeared.

The diagram showed how I could deactivate the two nukes on the other warships if I wanted to and I could activate any of the nukes I wanted.

So I disconnected the two ships with the innocent people onboard and I just looked at the commander who was still being pathetic.

"And then the Rex will have no choice than to accept me," he said.

"You're mad," I said.

The commander stormed over to me and pressed the gun into my mouth and I just smiled.

As I pressed the nuclear-arming button, I watched as the two innocent warships flew off to one side out of danger and I let the sheer deafening roar of the warning alarms echo around the bridge.

My ears started to bleed but I didn't care because

I had done my mission.

My mission was to always protect the Republic, protect my crew and save innocent people fleeing from the Imperium. My mum and dad had sacrificed their lives for me to do that and now I was sacrificing my life to save others.

I laughed as my life really was perfect and this was a great full-circle moment and as the panic reached the commander's eyes, I almost felt sorry for him.

He could have lived. We all could have lived but it was his delusions that made me do this.

As the nukes went off ripping the ship into thousands of shards and ripped my body to shreds I just grinned and hoped that my parents would be proud of me and I could finally be reunited with them.

Just like I had always wanted.

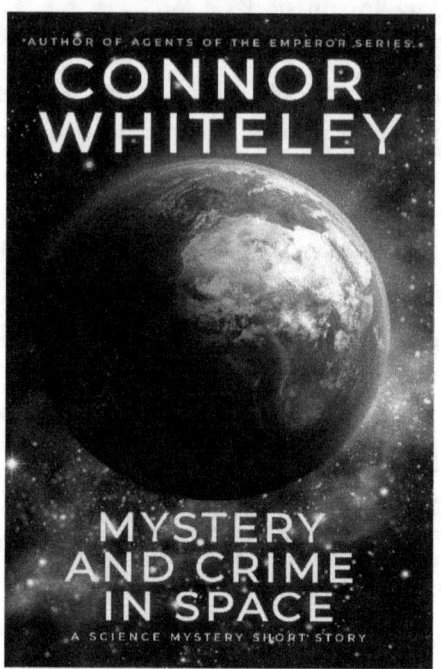

GET YOUR FREE SHORT STORY NOW!
And get signed up to Connor Whiteley's newsletter to hear about new gripping books, offers and exciting projects. (You'll never be sent spam)

https://www.subscribepage.io/garrosignup

WAY OF THE ODYSSEY SHORT STORY COLLECTION VOLUME 1

<u>About the author:</u>

Connor Whiteley is the author of over 60 books in the sci-fi fantasy, nonfiction psychology and books for writer's genre and he is a Human Branding Speaker and Consultant.

He is a passionate warhammer 40,000 reader, psychology student and author.

Who narrates his own audiobooks and he hosts The Psychology World Podcast.

All whilst studying Psychology at the University of Kent, England.

Also, he was a former Explorer Scout where he gave a speech to the Maltese President in August 2018 and he attended Prince Charles' 70th Birthday Party at Buckingham Palace in May 2018.

Plus, he is a self-confessed coffee lover!

Other books by Connor Whiteley:

Bettie English Private Eye Series

A Very Private Woman

The Russian Case

A Very Urgent Matter

A Case Most Personal

Trains, Scots and Private Eyes

The Federation Protects

Cops, Robbers and Private Eyes

Just Ask Bettie English

An Inheritance To Die For

The Death of Graham Adams

Bearing Witness

The Twelve

The Wrong Body

The Assassination Of Bettie English

Wining And Dying

Eight Hours

Uniformed Cabal

A Case Most Christmas

Gay Romance Novellas

Breaking, Nursing, Repairing A Broken Heart

Jacob And Daniel

Fallen For A Lie

Spying And Weddings

Clean Break

WAY OF THE ODYSSEY SHORT STORY COLLECTION VOLUME 1

Awakening Love
Meeting A Country Man
Loving Prime Minister
Snowed In Love
Never Been Kissed
Love Betrays You

<u>Lord of War Origin Trilogy:</u>
Not Scared Of The Dark
Madness
Burn Them All

<u>The Fireheart Fantasy Series</u>
Heart of Fire
Heart of Lies
Heart of Prophecy
Heart of Bones
Heart of Fate

<u>City of Assassins (Urban Fantasy)</u>
City of Death
City of Marytrs
City of Pleasure
City of Power

<u>Agents of The Emperor</u>
Return of The Ancient Ones
Vigilance
Angels of Fire
Kingmaker
The Eight
The Lost Generation
Hunt
Emperor's Council
Speaker of Treachery
Birth Of The Empire
Terraforma
Spaceguard

<u>The Rising Augusta Fantasy Adventure Series</u>
Rise To Power
Rising Walls
Rising Force
Rising Realm

<u>Lord Of War Trilogy (Agents of The Emperor)</u>
Not Scared Of The Dark
Madness
Burn It All Down

WAY OF THE ODYSSEY SHORT STORY COLLECTION VOLUME 1

<u>Miscellaneous:</u>
RETURN
FREEDOM
SALVATION
Reflection of Mount Flame
The Masked One
The Great Deer
English Independence

OTHER SHORT STORIES BY CONNOR WHITELEY

<u>Mystery Short Story Collections</u>
Criminally Good Stories Volume 1: 20 Detective Mystery Short Stories
Criminally Good Stories Volume 2: 20 Private Investigator Short Stories
Criminally Good Stories Volume 3: 20 Crime Fiction Short Stories
Criminally Good Stories Volume 4: 20 Science Fiction and Fantasy Mystery Short Stories
Criminally Good Stories Volume 5: 20 Romantic Suspense Short Stories

Mystery Short Stories:
Protecting The Woman She Hated
Finding A Royal Friend
Our Woman In Paris
Corrupt Driving
A Prime Assassination
Jubilee Thief
Jubilee, Terror, Celebrations
Negative Jubilation
Ghostly Jubilation
Killing For Womenkind
A Snowy Death
Miracle Of Death
A Spy In Rome
The 12:30 To St Pancreas
A Country In Trouble
A Smokey Way To Go
A Spicy Way To GO
A Marketing Way To Go
A Missing Way To Go
A Showering Way To Go
Poison In The Candy Cane
Kendra Detective Mystery Collection Volume 1
Kendra Detective Mystery Collection Volume 2
Mystery Short Story Collection Volume 1

WAY OF THE ODYSSEY SHORT STORY COLLECTION VOLUME 1

Mystery Short Story Collection Volume 2
Criminal Performance
Candy Detectives
Key To Birth In The Past

<u>Science Fiction Short Stories:</u>
Their Brave New World
Gummy Bear Detective
The Candy Detective
What Candies Fear
The Blurred Image
Shattered Legions
The First Rememberer
Life of A Rememberer
System of Wonder
Lifesaver
Remarkable Way She Died
The Interrogation of Annabella Stormic
Blade of The Emperor
Arbiter's Truth
Computation of Battle
Old One's Wrath
Puppets and Masters
Ship of Plague
Interrogation
Edge of Failure

Fantasy Short Stories:
City of Snow
City of Light
City of Vengeance
Dragons, Goats and Kingdom
Smog The Pathetic Dragon
Don't Go In The Shed
The Tomato Saver
The Remarkable Way She Died
Dragon Coins
Dragon Tea
Dragon Rider

All books in 'An Introductory Series':
Clinical Psychology and Transgender Clients
Clinical Psychology
Careers In Psychology
Psychology of Suicide
Dementia Psychology
Clinical Psychology Reflections Volume 4
Forensic Psychology of Terrorism And Hostage-Taking
Forensic Psychology of False Allegations
Year In Psychology
CBT For Anxiety
CBT For Depression
Applied Psychology

WAY OF THE ODYSSEY SHORT STORY COLLECTION VOLUME 1

BIOLOGICAL PSYCHOLOGY 3RD EDITION
COGNITIVE PSYCHOLOGY THIRD EDITION
SOCIAL PSYCHOLOGY- 3RD EDITION
ABNORMAL PSYCHOLOGY 3RD EDITION
PSYCHOLOGY OF RELATIONSHIPS- 3RD EDITION
DEVELOPMENTAL PSYCHOLOGY 3RD EDITION
HEALTH PSYCHOLOGY
RESEARCH IN PSYCHOLOGY
A GUIDE TO MENTAL HEALTH AND TREATMENT AROUND THE WORLD- A GLOBAL LOOK AT DEPRESSION
FORENSIC PSYCHOLOGY
THE FORENSIC PSYCHOLOGY OF THEFT, BURGLARY AND OTHER CRIMES AGAINST PROPERTY
CRIMINAL PROFILING: A FORENSIC PSYCHOLOGY GUIDE TO FBI PROFILING AND GEOGRAPHICAL AND STATISTICAL PROFILING.
CLINICAL PSYCHOLOGY
FORMULATION IN PSYCHOTHERAPY
PERSONALITY PSYCHOLOGY AND

INDIVIDUAL DIFFERENCES
CLINICAL PSYCHOLOGY
REFLECTIONS VOLUME 1
CLINICAL PSYCHOLOGY
REFLECTIONS VOLUME 2
Clinical Psychology Reflections Volume 3
CULT PSYCHOLOGY
Police Psychology

A Psychology Student's Guide To University
How Does University Work?
A Student's Guide To University And Learning
University Mental Health and Mindset

www.ingramcontent.com/pod-product-compliance
Lightning Source LLC
LaVergne TN
LVHW011855060526
838200LV00054B/4340